CONTENTS

1
BLACK LIGHTNING

Timothy Whistle had always been a clever boy. As a baby, there was nothing he enjoyed more than curling up in his cot with a good encyclopedia. The first words he spoke were the times tables. By the time he started at Moonwood County Primary School, he had already built his first computer, out of three egg boxes and a yoghurt carton.

Timothy Whistle had a wonderful future ahead of him. So why was he so unhappy? Simple. He had an enormous brain – but a ridiculously small body.

His arms and legs were like bits of string with knots where his knees and elbows should be. He was so skinny, he had once got lost in a crack in the sofa.

He could do sums that were a mile long and full of complicated signs and symbols – but he couldn't open a packet of crisps without collapsing, exhausted.

"Whistle, why are you so pathetic?" his teacher, Mr Jerkins, bellowed during the Friday PE lesson. "And stand up when I'm talking to you!"

"I *am* standing up," said Tim, sadly. "I'm just a very small person."

"Well DON'T be!" roared Mr Jerkins. "Get a move on and GROW, you miserable little slug! Grow big, strong and magnificent, like me! And while you're at it, do something about that weedy voice of yours! And grow a hair or two on your chest! Or if you can't grow your own, pinch some of your dad's!"

"I haven't got a dad," said Tim, miserably.

"Haven't got a dad, Whistle?" yelled Mr Jerkins. "Well it's about time you GOT one!"

Tim stared at the floor.

He hated PE and he hated Mr Jerkins. It was all right for *him*. *He* had a huge voice that practically caused earthquakes whenever he spoke. *His* chest was so hairy you could put plaits in it. And as for muscles ... there wasn't a single part of Mr Jerkins that didn't bulge with them.

Tim had never had a muscle in his life. He longed for a muscle or two. One on each arm would do. And that evening, as he walked home from school, he thought long and hard about how he might get some ...

Moonwood was quiet. Moonwood was *always* quiet. Or so Tim thought. But then, Tim was usually so deep in thought that he never noticed when anything *did* happen.

He didn't notice when odd Mr Dobbs galloped by, singing loudly, with a giggly Mrs Dobbs riding piggyback.

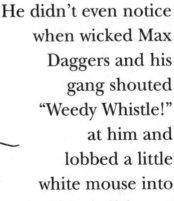

He didn't even notice when wicked Max Daggers and his gang shouted "Weedy Whistle!" at him and lobbed a little white mouse into the hood of his duffel coat.

Tim noticed nothing. And before
long, he was so lost in his vast brainful of
thoughts that he couldn't even
remember what he was supposed to be
thinking about ...

He arrived home to find his stepfather,
Ken Plankton, sprawling on the settee in
his pyjama trousers, burping.

Ken Plankton was a disgusting blob of
uselessness. He stank like an enormous
sweaty armpit. He hadn't
brushed his hair for
about ten years.
And he burped.
Spectacularly. He
was probably the
world's biggest
burper. It was all
he was good for.
That, and being
a lazy scruffbag.

"What are you doing here, you greasy little insect?" Ken Plankton snarled.

"I live here," sulked Tim.

"Can't you live somewhere else? You give me the creeps, you and that brain of yours. You ain't human. You're a little green alien, dressed in a Timothy Whistle costume."

"I can't help being clever," said Tim. "Just like you can't help being a slob."

"Clear off back to your own planet, you horrible alien," snapped Ken Plankton.

 "And take that Timothy Whistle costume off. Let's see what you really look like underneath . . . He grabbed Tim's ears and pulled hard.

Tim yelled. Then the little white mouse leapt out of the hood of his duffel coat and skittered away. Ken Plankton yelled.

Then Mum burst in.

"Ken! Are you trying to pull Timothy's face off again?" she sighed. "How many times have I told you? Timothy is *not* an alien."

Ken Plankton shrugged, and burped a long lazy burp.

Tim had to get outside. He couldn't bear to be in the same house as Ken Plankton. Thankfully, his new Captain Doom comic had arrived that morning. He took it from his schoolbag and stormed off into the garden.

Captain Doom was Tim's favourite superhero. He had loads of Captain

Doom comics, posters and toys. There was nothing Tim didn't know about Captain Doom, Warrior Lord of the Galaxy of Snig, and his faithful friend Disasterboy, and their everlasting fight against Balbosh the Slime King, Chief Disgustian of the Planet Nostrigore.

Tim longed to be like Captain Doom. Big, strong and full of awesome powers with which to destroy his enemies. But he knew that was impossible. Captain Doom had got his awesome powers from a mysterious bottle of Black Lightning – a gift from Grumblespit, Prince of the Pigpeople.

"Now, why can't somebody give *me* a gift like that?" Tim sighed. "Then I wouldn't be so ridiculously small ..."

And at that moment he noticed the words on the front of his Captain Doom comic:

FREE GIFT!!! SEE INSIDE!!!

Tim turned the page. And suddenly his ridiculously small body shivered with excitement ...

CONGRATULATIONS !!!
YOU HAVE WON A BOTTLE OF
BLACK LIGHTNING !!!
YES!!! YOU TOO CAN HAVE AWESOME
POWERS...
JUST LIKE CAPTAIN DOOM

The trouble was ... there was no bottle of Black Lightning. Just a picture of one. But before Tim had time to feel disappointed, he heard a strange noise.

A far-off whistling noise, that got louder ... and nearer ...

until, suddenly – Tim looked up, and something whizzed by him, so close that it almost set his nostrils on fire. Tim looked down again ... and gasped.

14

A diamond-shaped hole had burned right through his comic, where the picture of the Black Lightning had been.

Tim peered through the hole. And there, lying at his feet, all hot and smoky, was a tiny, black, diamond-shaped bottle.

"Black Lightning!" Tim cried. "A bottle of Black Lightning!"

2

Pyjama Man

The tiny diamond-shaped bottle was packed with black explosions. Dark waves swelled and surged, and purple fires flashed, no bigger than pinpricks.

"One mouthful of this ..." Tim whispered, " ... and my enemies will never torment me again."

But then he thought, "What if it melts my tongue? Or fries my insides? Or ... boils my enormous brain?"

His mind raced with a million awful things that might happen to him.

The bottle hummed in his hand, all the awesome power of the Black Lightning ready to burst out ...

And Tim couldn't stop himself.

He removed the glass stopper ... and drank.

Just one tiny drop.

"It tastes of ... STRAWBERRIES!" he exclaimed.

But then, something peculiar started happening inside him.

He felt as if his tongue was covered with creepy-crawlies. Tickly at first, but then prickly, and stingy, like a mouthful of poisonous spiders. He shivered huge, hard shivers. Hard enough to rattle his bones. Lumps popped up all over him and scuttled around under his skin. And suddenly, everything inside him was ablaze, and his whole body became a see-through skin full of bones and fire.

Tim was about to scream, when ... he was himself again. Except for a feeling of awesome power gathering inside him – and that strange taste on his tongue. A taste of strawberries ...

"I feel like a superhero!" he laughed. "A Strawberry-Flavoured Superhero!"

He took a deep breath. Now, he was ready. Now, Mr Jerkins would pay for all the horrible things he had ever done to Timothy Whistle. And as for Ken Plankton – after this night, he would never burp again ...

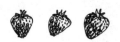

Exactly what happened that night, not even Tim knew for certain. But when he woke up the next morning, he knew that something *had* happened. Something extraordinary.

"Timothy Whistle!"

Mum's cry made him jump.

Tim tried to get out of bed, but he could barely move. He seemed to be inside a different body. One that was much too clumsy for him and full of stones.

"Timothy Whistle! Come here right now!"

Mum sounded cross with him. But why?

He felt terrible. His brain buzzed like a wasps' nest.

"Timothy Whistle, I'm waiting!" shrieked Mum.

Tim slowly stood up and tried to walk. But his legs didn't want to. He had to drag them across the floor, as if he were wearing concrete trousers.

"How DARE you!" shrieked Mum. She was standing by his bedroom door,

shaking with anger. "How DARE you do the dreadful things you did last night! Just LOOK what you did to your poor stepfather!" Ken Plankton appeared at Mum's shoulder.

At least, it *looked* like Ken Plankton. But something remarkable had happened to him. He was *properly dressed*. He wore a smart suit, with a crisp shirt and tie. His hair looked positively nice. And he smelled lovely. Ken Plankton wasn't a scruffbag any more.

"He burst into the bedroom like a wild animal!" he wailed. "He threatened to turn me into strawberry jam! And ... *look* what he did to me! He's made me look ... *elegant!* But worst of all ... " He held up a large jar. "He stole all my burps!"

He removed the lid, and some of the most disgusting noises ever made by a living creature poured out in a great torrent, like the ghastly gulps of a million monstrous toads.

Tim felt a sudden taste of strawberries on his tongue. He felt the tiny, black, diamond-shaped bottle, tucked neatly inside his pyjama pocket. Then he began to remember the things he had done last night.

The doorbell rang.

Ken Plankton scuttled off, as if terrified that someone might see him looking so presentable.

"I'll deal with you later, Timothy Whistle," Mum snapped, as she hurried downstairs to answer the door.

"Mrs Whistle? I need to speak with your Timothy about a very important matter..."

Tim recognised that voice.

He peered over the banister, and saw a very serious-looking Superintendent Brickhouse. And standing at his shoulder was... Mr Jerkins.

At least, it *looked* like Mr Jerkins. But he was all shrivelled and shrunken inside his big baggy tracksuit.

"Out of my way!" Mr Jerkins bellowed. Except ... it wasn't a bellow at all. It was a teeny-weeny squeak of a voice. "Where is he?! Let me get my hands on that pesky little pipsqueak!" He flailed his twig-like arms and waved his tiny fists furiously. "*Look* what he's done to me! I was having my early-morning jog when he came at me, like a maniac in stripy pyjamas! He threatened to turn me into strawberry jelly! Then he stole my voice, and all my muscles, and worst of all, he stole *this* ..."

He lifted his tracksuit top to reveal a smooth, pink chest. "My magnificent collection of chest hair! GONE!"

Mum gawped, horrifed.

"I'm sorry to have to ask you this, Mrs Whistle," Superintendent Brickhouse said gravely, "But who does your Timothy think he is? Pyjama Man?"

Tim could hold it in no longer. He just had to laugh. But it wasn't a Timothy-sized titter that came out. It was a huge booming bellow of a laugh. Mr Jerkins's laugh.

Now, Tim remembered everything.

He hurried back to his bedroom and looked at himself in his mirror.

His eyes had a strange, bright purple glow. And his stripy pyjamas seemed to be a hundred sizes too small. They stretched ... and strained ... and as buttons fired everywhere with a POP! POP! POP! ... they burst.

Muscles were bulging out all over him. Like massive boulders, crammed into every inch of his body, arms and neck. Mr Jerkins's muscles. And in the middle of Tim's chest was an awful lot of hair. Mr Jerkins's chest hair.

Tim was flabbergasted. His great brain told him it was scientifically impossible. But it was true.

"I did it! I really *am* a Strawberry-Flavoured Superhero!"

3

PURPLE FIRE

"Can I offer you tea and digestives? It's *so* nice to have guests," Mum said, as she led Superintendent Brickhouse and Mr Jerkins into the lounge. "Timothy Whistle! Downstairs! Right now! You've got some explaining to do!"

Tim tried to dress quickly, but with his little body stuffed full of Mr Jerkins's muscles, it was as easy as squeezing an elephant into a ballet dress. When he had finished, he looked as if someone had blown him up with a bicycle pump.

He crept downstairs as quietly as he could.

"I don't understand it," he heard Mum

saying, as he paused outside the lounge. "Perhaps he's just *borrowing* bits of Mr Jerkins. For scientific experiments. Timothy's a brilliant scientist. He's brilliant at most things."

"Is he, now?" Mr Jerkins squeaked, menacingly. "When I get my hands on him, we'll see how brilliant he is at begging for mercy..."

"No we won't," thought Tim. "I have *much* more important things to do..."

And he slipped out of the front door, then waddled off like a fat penguin towards Moonwood High Street.

People pointed at him and giggled, but he didn't care. He had never been happier in his life. He had vanquished his greatest enemies. And now, he would do what all superheroes did.

He would do good deeds. He would right wrongs. He would rid the streets of villainous fiends.

Tim waddled along the streets for hours. Annoyingly, all the villainous fiends seemed to have taken the day off. Everyone was perfectly well behaved.

Disappointed, Tim stopped at Trudge's Toffee Emporium. Max Daggers and his gang were there, eating jelly babies and causing trouble as usual. But Tim didn't notice them. He was lost in thought. He needed a new plan, and Mr Trudge's toffee always helped his massive brain to function.

A sudden loud voice made everyone jump.

"Attention, earthlings! We're looking for the Strawberry-Flavoured Superhero. Where is he?"

Two strange men had appeared from nowhere. They were dressed from head to toe in skin-tight purple and yellow bodysuits. One was tall and strong. The other was short and weedy, and wore two huge wristbands where tiny TV screens bleeped and flickered.

Tim stared, astounded.

It was Captain Doom and Disasterboy. Here, in Trudge's Toffee Emporium, on Moonwood High Street.

"Speak, Pitiful Creatures!" shouted Captain Doom, "Or I'll fill your trousers with cyberworms."

Everyone, including Tim, was too stunned to speak.

"Perhaps they don't speak our language, Captain Doom," said Disasterboy, fiddling with the knobs on one of his wristbands.

"Maybe they'll understand this: *Greetings, Human Bee Things. We come in peach. Where is the Slithery-Fingered Snooperhero?*" Nobody replied.

"What a pathetic planet this is, Disasterboy," sighed Captain Doom. "No intelligent life anywhere. Perhaps we should stop being nice to these Human Bee Things, and blast dirty great holes in them instead."

"Brilliant idea, Captain Doom!" exclaimed Disasterboy.

Max Daggers started sniggering.

"Oi! Weirdman! Do you know how stupid you look?" he sneered.

Captain Doom stared at him with blazing purple eyes. Then he raised a fist, and a thin bolt of purple fire crackled from it.

Suddenly, Max Daggers's jelly babies came to life. With blood-chilling shrieks, they leapt upon him. They pulled his hair, and plucked his eyebrows, and flapped his eyelids up and down, and wibbled his lips.

"Not as stupid as YOU," snarled Captain Doom.

Max Daggers staggered away, squealing. His gang ran off. Mr Trudge, meanwhile, hid under the counter and trembled.

"I–I am the Strawberry-Flavoured Superhero," Tim said, trying to sound superheroic.

Captain Doom turned his scary gaze upon him, and Tim gulped.

"We haven't much time," Captain Doom began. "Your city is in grave danger. Balbosh the Slime King may be here any moment. He knows you have a bottle of Black Lightning and he will do any disgusting thing to get it. Give it to me and I can protect it."

Tim reached for his pyjama pocket – then remembered he wasn't wearing his pyjamas.

"I … I left it at home," he said, sheepishly. "In my pyjama pocket."

"You've done WHAT?" hissed Captain Doom. "A priceless bottle of the most powerful thing in the universe? You left it *in your pyjama pocket?*"

"Yes," said Tim. And now, even Mr Jerkins's huge voice sounded small. "Sorry."

"Is this the most stupid planet in the universe or what?" Captain Doom demanded.

"No, Captain Doom," Disasterboy replied. "That'll be Ridiculus Five, in the Galaxy of Idiotica. I should know. It's where I come from."

"Hang on a minute ..." said Tim, starting to use his brain at last. "How did *you* know I had the Black Lightning? And how did you know I'd be here, in Trudge's Toffee Emporium?"

"I'm a superhero," boomed Captain Doom. "I'm *supposed* to know things."

"So why didn't you know I'd left the Black Lightning at home?"

"Ah. Well. All superheroes must have *something* they're not very good at," said Captain Doom. "It says so in the *Superheroes Instruction Manual.*

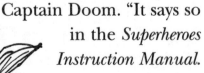

We're not allowed to be invincible. It isn't
fair to our enemies. And it so happens that
I'm not very good at remembering things.
I've got a magnificent forgettory. But my
remembory is useless."

Tim was amazed.

"And what about Disasterboy?" he
asked. "What is he not very good at?"

One of Disasterboy's wristbands
suddenly began to
bleep. He jumped,
and sent a jar
of gobstoppers
spraying across
the floor.

"He's not very good at anything," said
Captain Doom.

"It's Balbosh, Captain Doom," said
Disasterboy. "He's in the area..."

"Are you sure?"

"This thing on my arm's making bleepy noises, Captain Doom. What else could it mean?"

"Balbosh *must not* find that bottle of Black Lightning," Captain Doom said, firmly. "Only I can stop him."

He stared hard at Tim.

"But I'll need your help …"

Tim's eyes sparkled and his heart leapt.

4

THE SLIME KING

Soon, Tim was waddling through the streets of Moonwood beside two real live superheroes. Small children followed them, thinking they were clowns from a travelling circus. Others crossed the road to avoid them. Everyone else just stared.

A man was painting the door of Drizzle's Hairdressers. He stared so hard, he painted the woman coming out of the door instead. She didn't notice. She was staring so hard, she put her dog on her head, and took her hat for a walk.

As they walked, Tim told Captain Doom what he had done to Mr Jerkins and Ken Plankton the night before.

Captain Doom roared with laughter.

"I remember the first time I used *my* awesome powers," he said. "I was hopeless. I accidentally turned my mother's hair into poisonous snakes."

"That's terrible," said Tim.

"Well, I got lucky. She *loved* having poisonous-snake hair. Said it was the best

hairstyle she'd ever had. Brushing it was a bit of a nightmare, though …"

Just then, a scream rang down Milkjug Road. Disasterboy's wristbands flashed. Sirens wailed. Alarms rang.

"It's Balbosh! He's close!"

Up ahead, terrified shoppers gathered on the pavement.

"That's Blunderwood's Supermarket!" Tim cried. "My mum works there!"

"That's where the Black Lightning is," said Disasterboy. "Your mother found it in your pyjama pocket after you sneaked out this morning. She took it to work with her."

"How do you know that?" asked Captain Doom.

"Oh, I knew that ages ago," said Disasterboy, pointing to one of his wristbands. "It said so here on my little computer thingy."

"THEN WHY DIDN'T YOU TELL ME?" scolded Captain Doom.

"You never asked," shrugged Disasterboy.

"We're too late..." Captain Doom cried. "Balbosh has already found the Black Lightning..."

"But...but what about Mum?" Tim asked, suddenly terrified.

"Oh, Balbosh will have dissolved her in a giant green gloop of everlasting disgustingness," Captain Doom sighed. "Sorry, kid. These things happen."

Tim's head swam with horrible thoughts.

"NO!" he cried.

And off he ran towards Blunderwood's Supermarket, Captain Doom and Disasterboy chasing behind him.

Superintendent Brickhouse was already there, waving his loudspeaker.

"It came out of nowhere!" someone wept. "It was disgusting! Ugly and slimy, like a frog monster!"

"It touched me!" squealed another. "It had horrible sucky fingers, like an octopus creature!"

"Let me through!" boomed Captain Doom. "I'm a superhero!"

Captain Doom, Disasterboy and Tim burst into the supermarket. It was deserted now, and strangely quiet.

Slowly, they crept past the tinned foods ... and the bread and cakes ... and the breakfast cereals ...

Then Tim looked up ... and saw the most gruesome sight.

An almighty dollop of green slime hung down from a high rafter, like something that had been blown from a gigantic nose. It just dangled there, looking as if it might plop to the ground at any moment.

And trapped inside it was Mum. She screamed, but no one heard her. She kicked and punched against the slippery green walls, but she couldn't break free.

"The giant green gloop of everlasting disgustingness!" Tim gasped. "When I get my hands on Balbosh the Slime King, I'll ... I'll ... "

"You'll use your awesome powers against me?" asked a dark, gurgly voice. "I think not."

Balbosh was suddenly standing in their path. At the very sight of him, Tim's muscles twitched, itching for a fight.

Balbosh the Slime King looked like a disgustingly fat man squeezed into the body of a hideous lizard. He had a huge head with a big boggly eye on either side of it. His mouth seemed to stretch on and on, for ever, and a thin, poisonous tongue flicked menacingly between his dribbly lips. His skin was greeny-grey,

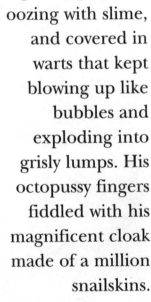

oozing with slime, and covered in warts that kept blowing up like bubbles and exploding into grisly lumps. His octopussy fingers fiddled with his magnificent cloak made of a million snailskins.

"Let my mum go," Tim snarled.

"Ooh, temper, temper," smiled Balbosh. "No, thank you very much, I won't. She was a very naughty girl. She wouldn't give me this ..."

Triumphantly, he held up a tiny diamond-shaped bottle.

"Even though I asked her *ever* so nicely. Amazing, the things people leave in their pyjama pockets. Eh, Mr Strawberry-Flavoured Superhero?"

"Go ahead and drink it!" smirked Captain Doom. "I hate to disappoint you ... but THAT isn't *real* Black Lightning! It's a cheap copy! The universe is full of them! You've been cheated, Balbosh! You'll NEVER have awesome powers like me!"

Balbosh laughed a sickeningly gurgly laugh.

"Dear me, Captain Doom! You of all people, telling porkie pies! I hate to disappoint you, but, you see, I already *have* drunk it. Just one tiny drop. And guess what? I really *have* got awesome powers, *just* like you!"

"You'll never be as powerful as me, you slithering heap of nostril droppings!" Captain Doom roared, his purple eyes blazing.

"Let's find out, shall we?" snapped Balbosh.

And the fight began ...

5

RED RAIN

Captain Doom hurled a fistful of purple fire. But, incredibly, as it struck Balbosh, all it did was turn to purple smoke. And when the smoke had cleared, Balbosh was soaring in the air above them in a flying shopping trolley. Full of groceries.

From the shopping trolley, Balbosh hurled down three tins of baked beans, four large pizzas, a bunch of bananas, a box of eggs and a huge plucked turkey. The tins hit the ground and exploded. Baked beans burst out and swarmed around Captain Doom like angry bees. The bananas peeled off their skins and tossed them under Captain Doom's feet.

He slipped and slithered, and as he fell, a dozen eggs cracked themselves open all over his face and started frying.

"Disasterboy, get these groceries off me!" he screamed.

But Disasterboy had his own problems. The pizzas were attacking him like a squadron of alien spaceships, and the turkey had landed smack on top of him. He struggled to wrestle his head out of its bottom, but couldn't.

It was up to Tim now. This was the moment he had longed for. A chance to show the world that he was no longer the boy with the planet-sized brain, but the body of a stick insect.

He took a deep breath, gathered all his awesome powers, and hurled an enormous purple ball of flame. It exploded all over Balbosh … and fizzled away to nothingness.

Then, catastrophe struck.

Balbosh dive-bombed, and heaved
six huge Stilton cheeses over the side
of his flying trolley. They hit the ground

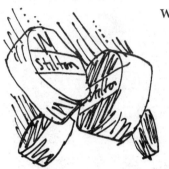

with terrible splats and
the most poisonous
pongs ever created.
Captain Doom and
Tim held their faces
and coughed until
their throats burned.

Balbosh just laughed a nasty, shrieky
laugh and flew away.

"He's DisGUSTing ...!" spluttered Tim.
"AND he's got as much awesome power as
we have! We'll *never* beat him! Unless ..."

Tim spotted something on the supermarket shelves.

His magnificent brain flickered into life. "That's it!" he cried.

Within seconds he had worked out a brilliant plan ...

"Captain Doom, what is the one single thing that Balbosh is afraid of?" he asked.

Captain Doom thought.

"I can't remember ... "

"Yes, you can! Think!"

"I can't! My remembory's gone and my forgettory's forgotten!"

"*Red Rain!*" he exclaimed. "I read it once in a Captain Doom comic, a bottle of Red Rain will melt Balbosh down to a stinking puddle of frothy green sludge ... "

"But Red Rain doesn't exist!" moaned Captain Doom. "I've searched the entire universe for it! There's no such thing!"

"Isn't there?" said Tim, his eyes shining excitedly.

From the supermarket shelf behind him, he seized a fat glass bottle full of a bright red liquid. Captain Doom gasped. "BALBOSH!" boomed Tim. "I've got some Red Rain here! Surrender – or perish!" There was no answer. But then there was a clattering sound as Balbosh's shopping trolley landed in the bakery section.

Balbosh appeared around the end of the aisle, striding towards them on his squelchy, lizardy feet. He stared straight at Tim, his big boggly eyes blazing with rage, his horrible exploding skin awash with slime.

FRESH BREAD

"You're teasing me," he said. "Red Rain? Here? I don't think so."

"Why not? You found the bottle of Black Lightning here, didn't you? Well, there's Red Rain here, too. So, let my mum go before I blast you with it."

Balbosh blinked. Then he laughed.

"Oh, what an excellent joke! For a moment, I almost believed you! How amusing you are, Strawberry Boy!"

Tim held his breath. Would his daring plan work?

He aimed the fat glass bottle at Balbosh. It began to throb and burn in his hand. Then, with an enormous SWOOOSH! the Red Rain fired out and splattered all over the Slime King.

"*NO-O-O-O-O-O-O-O-O-O-O-O-O-O-O-O-O-O-!*"
Balbosh screeched.

In panic, he shot out his long tongue,
like a poison arrow, straight at Tim's head.

Tim shut his eyes
and screwed up his
face into a tight
little ball.

But nothing
happened
to him.

There was
a disgusting
popping
plopping
noise, and
a horrendous gurgle, like the
sound of thick custard being sucked
down a plughole. There was a long,
loud hiss, and a ghastly burp that Ken
Plankton would have been proud of. And
then ... silence.

Tim opened his eyes again.

All that was left of Balbosh was a sticky green mess on the supermarket floor ... and a tiny, black, diamond-shaped bottle.

Captain Doom picked it up, his fried-eggy, baked-beany face frozen in shock.

"*Tiiiim! Heeeeelp!*"

The giant green gloop of everlasting disgustingness melted away, and Mum tumbled from the high rafters of the supermarket ... straight into Captain Doom's arms.

Several tons of green gunk landed on top of Disasterboy.

"You're safe now, ma'am," said Captain Doom. "Balbosh is destroyed."

"It wasn't *real* Red Rain ..." smiled Tim. "But Balbosh didn't know that..."

Captain Doom took the fat glass bottle and read the label.

"*Strawberry Sauce. The perfect dessert topping idea...* And pretty good at melting Slime Kings too!"

"You tricked Balbosh!" said Disasterboy, finally managing to wrench his head out of the huge turkey's bottom. "You destroyed him with Strawberry Sauce! That makes you ... THE STRAWBERRY SORCERER!"

"No," said Tim. "I just used my brains. That's all."

6
THE ALMIGHTY BURP

That evening after tea, Tim looked around at Mum, Ken Plankton and Mr Jerkins, and found it hard to believe the strange things that had happened to them that day.

"It's a shame Captain Doom and Disasterboy couldn't stop for tea," said Mum.

"They had to go. They've got a whole galaxy to look after," said Tim.

"Still. It was good of them to turn you all back to your normal selves before they left," Mum smiled.

"Was it?" spat Ken Plankton, chomping a huge slab of chocolate cake disgustingly.

"*I* don't feel like my normal self." He burped. "I used to burp *much* louder than that."

Tim scowled at Ken Plankton. He almost wished he could be the Strawberry Sorcerer again, and blast Ken Plankton out of his chair, and splatter him over the wall above the fireplace. He smiled at the idea. But not for long. He knew now that his own brain was the only awesome power he would ever need.

"Thank you for a marvellous tea,
Mrs Whistle!" Mr Jerkins bellowed in his
huge voice.

He got up to leave, and couldn't resist
stroking his wonderful collection of
chest hair lovingly, like a pet that was lost
and was now found again. (He had all
his muscles back, too, except for two
little ones. Tim had kept them – one on
each arm.) "I'm off to do some training!
Being nasty to small boys takes a lot of
hard work!"

"Lovely to see you," Mum smiled. "It's nice to have guests. Isn't it, Ken?"

"Absolutely dee–BURP!–lightful."

Tim ran off to his room to do some thinking. He'd had an idea for a magnificent spaceship, powered by all the green vegetables that no one ever ate in the Moonwood County Primary School canteen.

It would be fast enough to carry Tim all the way to Mars, and still have him back in school before afternoon playtime …

Tim's deepest thoughts were interrupted by a huge explosion that rocked the entire house. An explosion that sounded remarkably like ... Ken Plankton. Burping.

Tim ran downstairs to the lounge and ... He froze. Ken Plankton's burp had devastated the whole room. It had blasted Ken Plankton clean off the sofa; and splattered him, groaning, over the wall above the fireplace.

Mum was holding a tiny, black, diamond-shaped bottle. Her eyes glowed bright purple ...

"There you are, Ken," she said. "Thanks to my awesome powers, you can now burp as loud as you like."

Madcap Moonwood

By Adrian Boote
Illustrated by Tim Archbold

Madcap Moonwood books are available from all good bookshops,
or can be ordered direct from the publisher:
Orchard Books, PO BOX 29, Douglas IM99 1BQ
Credit card orders please telephone 01624 836000 or fax 01624 837033
or e-mail: bookshop@enterprise.net for details.

To order please quote title, author and ISBN and your full name and address.
Cheques and postal orders should be made payable to 'Bookpost plc'.
Postage and packing is FREE within the UK
(overseas customers should add £1.00 per book).

Prices and availability are subject to change.